Lisa M.Cottrell-Bentley

Wright on Time:
South Dakota

Illustrated by Tanja Bauerle

Printed in the United States of America

First Printing, 2011

ISBN: 0-9824829-5-7
ISBN-13: 978-0-9824829-5-7
Library of Congress Control Number: 2011925417

Do Life Right, Inc.
P.O. Box 61
Sahuarita, AZ 85629

Visit www.WrightOnTimeBooks.com to order additional copies
or e-mail sales@wrightontimebooks.com to inquire about bulk and
wholesale discounts.

Flat Aidan and Flat Nadia
have made it to South Dakota!

Color and travel with your own Flat Aidan and Flat Nadia which you can get from the back of this book or download from **www.WrightOnTimeBooks.com**!

Dedicated to my parents,
Tim and Marsha,
who believed in me before anyone else in the world. They are
the greatest grandparents I could ever have imagined for my own
children, and the Wright children's loving grandparents are
based on them.

SOUTH DAKOTA

South Dakota became a State
on November 2nd, 1889

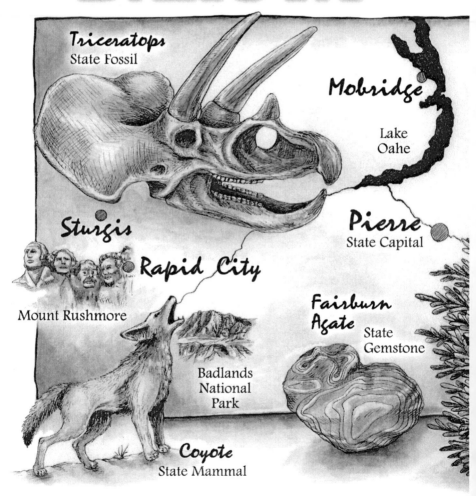

Triceratops
State Fossil

Mobridge

Lake
Oahe

Sturgis

Rapid City

Mount Rushmore

Pierre
State Capital

Fairburn Agate
State
Gemstone

Badlands
National
Park

Coyote
State Mammal

Mount Rushmore State

State Nickname

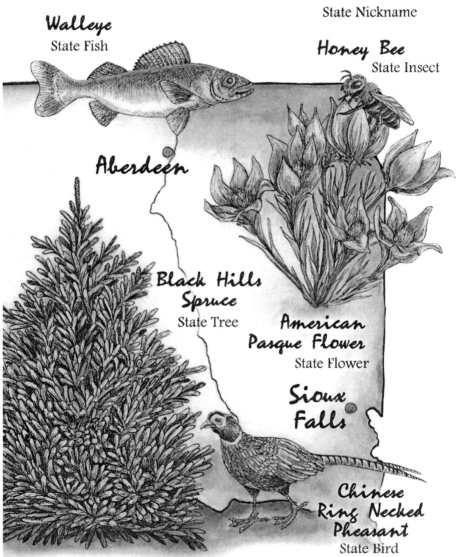

Walleye
State Fish

Honey Bee
State Insect

Aberdeen

Black Hills Spruce
State Tree

American Pasque Flower
State Flower

Sioux Falls

Chinese Ring Necked Pheasant
State Bird

Chapter One

Prince Pumpkin the Third took a hesitant step across the big green pillow. His footing was unsure, but he saw a pea in the distance and he was hungry.

The Wright family was taking a nap. They'd had a long drive with no rest stops from Western Wyoming to the Black Hills in South Dakota. Their RV had been broken down for more than two weeks and the replacement engine part had finally come in. With the Recreational

Wright 🐢n Time

Vehicle in working order, the family was anxious to get on the road. They'd been living in the RV parked in a parking lot for over a week and they were excited at the prospect of getting running water and a proper shower or bath again. The campground they stayed at the previous week had been no better since it had a broken well pump.

Harrison and Stephanie, the parents, had alternated driving straight through the night. It was now early morning. The RV and towed car were securely parked in a campground on the south side of the Black Hills. Being freshly showered, they'd all decided to take a short nap before tackling the new day.

But someone had forgotten to put the little turtle back in his terrarium. Prince Pumpkin the Third didn't mind. He was enjoying his private adventure. Up he stepped again, determined to climb the mini-mountain until he got to his prize.

It was shaping up to be a hot and muggy August day. The temperature in the RV was rising quickly. Aidan, the seven year old boy, had sweat dripping down his forehead and his brown curls were damp. He wiped his face on his green pillow and rolled over. Nadia, the eleven year old girl, pulled her long red hair off her sweaty neck and pushed her sheet off her legs. The kids were napping on their kitchen table, converted into a nice double-sized bed. They liked sleeping there sometimes when their bunks were being used for storage.

The motions of the children knocked Prince Pumpkin the Third off his footing and he slipped from Aidan's green pillow to Nadia's blue one. He didn't mind, since it took him several inches closer to the pea. He paused briefly to make sure all four of his feet were solidly on the pillow and then he continued on his journey.

It was hard work, but the pea got closer with every step. Prince Pumpkin the Third stepped over the girl's golden red hair and edged his way to the end of the pillow.

Nadia's hand moved slightly as Prince Pumpkin the Third's foot tickled her. Asleep, she wiggled her fingers. A black and bronze device fell from her hand directly in front of the turtle.

Chapter Two

"Where's Prince Pumpkin the Third?" Aidan asked, as he groggily peered into the turtle's habitat. The terrarium was tightly secured to the edge of the kitchen counter, so the turtle would be safe during their travels. "He's not in here."

The boy's worried tone woke Nadia. "Huh?" she asked, rubbing her eyes.

"Prince Pumpkin the Third is not in his home," Aidan cried. "Oh, no! I forgot to put him back in after our showers. I was so excited to get him clean water and food, and to let him wander around…" his voice trailed off.

Nadia bolted up. "He must be here somewhere."

The two began looking around, careful not to move anything without looking first. They didn't want to accidentally hurt the little guy.

"What if he got out of the RV while we were sleeping?" Nadia asked.

"What if we rolled over on top of him?" Aidan asked. "I'm pretty sure I had him in bed with me."

"Let's start looking there, then."

Nadia slowly gathered the sheets, making sure the turtle wasn't in them, and laid them to the side.

Aidan gently lifted his green pillow and moved it to the sheet pile. "Wow, it's hot in here," he said as he wiped his forehead with the back of his hand.

Nadia looked under the make-shift bed. "Not here."

"Oh, no!" Aidan screamed.

SOUTH DAKOTA

Aidan had found the little turtle. Prince Pumpkin the Third was frozen in place, clutching the Time Tuner with his front two legs. His eyes looked glassy.

"Prince Pumpkin!" the two children cried as they touched the little turtle.

Aidan's scream woke their parents, who came running from the little bedroom to see what was wrong.

"It's Prince Pumpkin the Third," Nadia cried to her parents. "He's... he's... he's..." she sputtered.

"I didn't mean to leave him out of his home," Aidan cried.

"Let's see," Harrison said as he bent down to look at the little turtle.

"Is he dead?" Nadia asked. She turned away from the scene as tears rolled down her face. Stephanie hugged her daughter and patted her consolingly on the back.

"I killed him!" Aidan screamed. "It's all my fault." Stephanie reached across and rubbed Aidan's back as well.

Wright 🐢 n Time

Harrison picked up the turtle. The Time Tuner—a strange device the Wrights had found in a cave in Arizona—was stuck in the turtle's grasp.

"He isn't looking so good," Harrison agreed.

Stephanie looked at the scene and quizzically shot up her eyebrows. She was still holding Nadia in a standing hug. Tears were coming to her eyes too. Prince Pumpkin the Third had always been in her life. He had joined her family before she was even born. She pushed her short blonde hair off her face. The heat was getting to them all. She blinked and a tear rolled down her face.

Harrison sat on the edge of the bed and gingerly set the turtle in his lap. Prince Pumpkin the Third hadn't blinked once.

Aidan knelt on the floor. "Oh, please be alive," he gently whispered into the turtle's ears.

Stephanie and Nadia stood perfectly still as they both looked at Prince Pumpkin the Third.

Harrison carefully took the device out of the turtle's stiff grasp and set it on Nadia's pillow. He started to sigh. It looked like the turtle had breathed his last breath.

"Prince Pumpkin the Third lived a long, long life," Stephanie started to say, when all of a sudden, the turtle blinked.

The turtle raised his neck up high as if saying, "Pet me!"

The whole family laughed and shrieked in delight.

"He's not dead!" Aidan squealed. "That's freaky awesome!"

"He's okay!" Nadia cried. Tears of happiness now fell down her face, left over from the sad tears welling in her eyes moments before.

Harrison and Stephanie looked at each other in confusion. They'd never seen anything like it in their whole lives.

"What just happened there?" Stephanie asked.

"I don't know," Harrison said. "But I'm sure happy this little guy's fine." He turned to the turtle.

Wright 🐢n Time

Aidan and Nadia were alternating stroking the turtle's neck just the way Prince Pumpkin the Third liked it.

"I bet he's hungry," Aidan said. He rushed away to get the turtle some food.

"We should probably put him somewhere safe," Stephanie said as she took over Aidan's stroking duties.

Prince Pumpkin the Third saw the food in Aidan's hand and he started to clamber out of Harrison's lap. The children giggled in delight. Nadia got out of Aidan's way as the boy took the food straight to the turtle.

Nadia sat next to Harrison and watched the turtle eat. After he ate a few peas, a chopped carrot piece, and a whole leaf of lettuce, she got up to get the turtle some water.

"It's so much fun to watch him eat," Stephanie said.

"He's starving!" Aidan said. "He still seems hungry and he's already eaten more than he usually eats in one whole day."

"I'll get him some more," Nadia said. She handed Aidan a little bowl of water and went back to get more peas, Prince Pumpkin the Third's favorite food.

After she handed Aidan the rest of the food, Nadia sat on the bed again. She glanced around and noticed the device on her pillow. "Weird that Prince Pumpkin the Third was holding the Time Tuner," she said. The Wrights had seen the Time Tuner do some amazing things since they had found it, but they were still trying to figure out exactly what it was for and where it was from. In Utah, they discovered that it could power electronic devices like computers. In Wyoming, they found that it had the power to grow plants. The whole thing seemed very strange and mysterious.

Nadia picked up the device and examined it. At a glance, it looked the same black and bronze as it almost always did. Yet, Nadia knew every curve and speck of the pictograms which were usually on the device. She immediately knew something was different. The pictograms had shifted and changed spots. There was also a new pictogram below the usual ones. It sort of looked like a turtle at first glance, but not quite like the original turtle that was on the device when they'd found it in Arizona.

"Look!" Nadia called out. "The device is different!"

Harrison stood and put the turtle into his terrarium. Prince Pumpkin the Third immediately walked around his little home.

"Let's see," Stephanie said.

Nadia held it up to show her parents while Aidan sat next to the turtle and whispered, "I'm so sorry, Prince Pumpkin the Third. I'll never leave you unattended again."

Prince Pumpkin the Third was making more noise than he'd ever made. He was wriggling and his tail was even wagging. He was a happy turtle.

"He looks somehow younger," Aidan said.

Stephanie regarded the turtle. "He does. More vibrant and his shell's a bit shinier."

Aidan continued playing with the turtle, who in turn was being quite playful himself.

Nadia got her notebook out and hurried to copy down the symbols on the Time Tuner before they were gone. She had seen the device change before, but she had no idea what caused it to change.

"I'm going to e-mail these to Maeve right away," she said. Maeve Smith was a friend of theirs and an expert on languages.

"Good idea!" Harrison said.

While Nadia was holding the device, Harrison opened the windows in their home, hoping for a cross breeze to lessen the rising heat. He glanced at his watch and realized it was almost noon already, but at least that would mean the main heat of the day would be passing soon.

An alarm went off, and Harrison groaned. "Oh, I've forgotten in all the excitement. We have an appointment this afternoon. We've got to get going."

Chapter Three

"I'm also bringing my laptop," Nadia said. She was happy her grandparents had express mailed her laptop and Aidan's from home. She now had unlimited access to all her personal notes and computer files without needing to time-share with other people in her family. That had been too hard on all of them.

"Okay," Harrison said. "I've got everything else we'll need for the day."

Wright 🐢n Time

The Black Hills area reminded the Wrights of the other mountains they'd seen so far on their trip. Stephanie, a serious amateur photographer, enjoyed photographing the rolling hills. As she snapped pictures, she wondered why they weren't called the Black Mountains, since they were so large. On the other hand, she mused, the land did roll more than the other mountain areas they'd been to.

"Look!" Aidan said, as they turned a sharp corner. "Cool motorcycle."

Harrison snuck a smile to Stephanie. As usual, he was behind the wheel so that Stephanie could take photographs while they drove.

Nadia glanced up from her note taking. She had the Time Tuner in one hand and a pen in the other, with a notebook on her lap. "Missed it," she said to Aidan. "Sorry."

"It was a cool one, too. It was bright orange with flames on the side," he said to his sister.

"Look, another." Nadia pointed out her window.

SOUTH DAKOTA

"This would be a freaky awesome place to ride a motorcycle," Aidan said as he stared at the yellow Harley-Davidson passing their car. "It has a picture on the side. I can't tell what it is, but it sort of looks like the Grand Canyon."

A new pack of motorcycles passed them by. The blacks, reds, and blues of their paint jobs blurred as they roared past.

"Wow! What is going on?" Aidan asked as yet another pack of motorcycles, this time green with shooting stars on their gas tanks, passed them.

"It's like we've entered motorcycle heaven or something," Nadia said.

"More like hog heaven," Stephanie said as she glanced at her kids in the backseat.

"Hog?" the two kids asked simultaneously.

"Yeah, people often call Harley-Davidson motorcycles *hogs*."

"Why?" Nadia said.

"I think it's because Harley-Davidson motorcycle owners are part of an association called the 'Harley Owners Group'. It forms the acronym HOG, like *hog*," Stephanie told her.

"Grandpa and Grandma's motorcycles are hogs," Aidan laughed. "They're definitely not cows."

"But, Grandma's is!" Nadia said. "Hers is painted like a black and white Holstein cow with little sunflowers on the bottom."

"Too true!" he laughed. "I guess hers is a cow-hog!"

"Grandpa's has the solar system on it. Good thing he only has the first few planets. It would have been a lot of work to repaint Pluto off of it."

"Even if Pluto isn't a planet anymore, it still exists," Harrison said from the front seat. "It's still the same size and all, just called a dwarf planet."

Several more packs of motorcycles zoomed past. Aidan tried to see them all, but he couldn't quite make out all the fancy designs.

"I bet there is a famous painter or something here," he finally said. "These motorcycles are all so fancy."

They came around a long curve and a town appeared in the distance. They drove another

SOUTH DAKOTA

fifteen minutes, curving through the hills. The further they drove, the more motorcycles they saw. They also saw thousands of tents in the flatter grassland prairie areas and, as they neared the town, in the front and back yards of every house in sight. Aidan gaped out his window. He was in awe of all the people and motorcycles. Soon they entered the actual town. An unimposing white sign said, "Sturgis, South Dakota."

They continued driving on the highway towards Main Street, which had hundreds of thousands of motorcycles sitting mere centimeters apart, with what looked to be many more thousands of people milling about. Hundreds, if not thousands, of vendor stalls with large signs advertising everything from funnel cakes to turquoise jewelry and famous Black Hills gold at "the best prices" to fake and real tattoos filled the sides. The children stared out the windows wide-eyed.

"What's going on?" Nadia asked.

"You'll see," Stephanie said.

Wright 🐢n Time

The street ahead glittered from the sunlight hitting chrome, and they all reflexively squinted. Harrison took a quick right before the car reached the hubbub. Two more quick zips and they pulled up into the driveway of a small red brick house with bushes and purple and white flowers lining the front.

As the car pulled up, three figures ran out of the house to greet the family. Two were recognizable.

As the Wrights got out of their car, hugs covered the children.

"Grandma! Grandpa!" Nadia and Aidan hollered. "What are you doing here?"

"Surprise!" Grandma and Grandpa said in unison. Huge smiles covered their gleaming faces.

SOUTH DAKOTA

Chapter Four

"Hi, I'm Billie," a pretty blonde young woman said to the family. "I already feel like I know all of you. Your grandparents have told me so much about you kids. Come on inside and have a cool drink." She smiled at the children.

They walked through the front door into the living room.

Wright 🐢 n Time

"Hi, I'm Bobbie," an identical woman said as she entered the living room from the kitchen carrying a large tray of glasses full of lemonade.

"We're twins," they said, bobbing their heads and talking in an identical fashion. They were both wearing red, white, and blue T-shirts with eagles on the front. They had on jeans and hiking boots. Billie's hair was pulled into a ponytail and Bobbie's was braided. If not for that, no one would have been able to tell them apart.

"Freaky, freaky cool!" Aidan said. "I've never met twins before."

"This is Billie and Bobbie's house," Grandma said.

"I've known their dad for years," Grandpa said. "We worked together."

"After our trip to South Dakota a couple of weeks ago, we ran into Billie and her dad in Tucson. We told them about our frustration at not getting to see you all," Grandma said.

"And one thing led to another," Billie said.

Bobbie started handing out the glasses of icy lemonade. Each had a slice of real lemon on the side with a flexible white straw sticking out the top.

"And, I mentioned how Harrison had lost that writing job he was supposed to do about families vacationing in South Dakota," Grandpa said. "Mmm, this is good!" he added as he took a long sip of lemonade.

"Homemade," Bobbie said proudly.

"I can tell." Grandpa smiled.

"And I mentioned how my sister, Bobbie," Billie pointed even though it wasn't even slightly necessary, "was looking for a journalist for an article on the Sturgis Motorcycle Rally."

"I get that this town is Sturgis, but what's a rally?" Aidan asked.

"A rally is when people come together for a common reason. Here, there is a yearly motorcycle rally known as the Sturgis Motorcycle Rally. Everyone is here to learn more about motorcycles and to have fun showing off their own bikes. Most everyone here has Harley-Davidson bikes, which is a special kind," Harrison told his son.

Wright ❉n Time

"Freaky cool! That's why we saw so many motorcycles on the road!"

"Yes!" Stephanie said.

"See?" Harrison said. "Everything always works out perfectly!" He'd been having a hard time keeping the surprise reunion a secret from his children, but the looks on their faces were well worth the wait.

Stephanie smiled at Harrison. She loved how upbeat he always was.

"So when are you guys headed home? Isn't school about to start?" Bobbie asked the family.

"We're not going back home to Tucson permanently for nearly four years!" Harrison said.

"What?" Billie asked.

"What about school for the kids?" Bobbie asked.

Nadia laughed. "We're homeschoolers…"

"Actually *roadschoolers* since we live on the road now!" Aidan said proudly.

"That sounds really fun!" said Bobbie.

"It's freaky fun!" Aidan agreed.

SOUTH DAKOTA

"Speaking of homeschooling families," Stephanie said to her parents. "Martin and Robin just had their baby a few days ago."

"It's a girl. They've named her Raven Ann Wright," Nadia added.

"I've been wondering about them," Grandma said. "I'd love to see some new photographs of all your nieces and nephew."

"Martin is Harrison's brother," Stephanie said to Bobbie and Billie so they would know who was being talked about. "We're going to be seeing them in October when we're in Iowa. They have a farm there, as well as a small home near ours in Arizona. Both their house and ours are being rented, though. Robin wanted to be near her extended family when their new baby was born."

"I can't wait to meet little Raven," Nadia said. "She's so cute in the pictures!"

"You'll have to show me!" Grandma said, smiling at Nadia.

Seeing their grandparents was such a surprise, the Wright children could not stay still. Smiles were plastered on their faces and they kept jumping up and down. Nadia kept whispering into her grandma's ear, then running to whisper into her grandpa's.

"How long are you staying here?" Nadia finally asked out loud. "We're going to be in South Dakota for a whole month, although we'll only be in this area for a week and a half. We're also going to the Badlands and Mitchell to see the corn palace. Are you going to come, too?"

"Yeah, are you?" Aidan asked, pulling on his grandpa's arm.

"And we'll hopefully go to Wind Cave so I can see the boxwork speleogens," Nadia added. "Those are like the speleothems we saw in Arizona but they aren't made from dripping water. They are made from erosion and look like huge honeycombs."

"You're interested in caves and geology?" asked Billie, recognizing the terms for cave formations.

Nadia nodded.

"Well, I've got some things to show you later that I think you'll really like!"

"Cool!"

SOUTH DAKOTA

"You're not letting them answer the question," Aidan interrupted. "How long are you going to be with us?"

"We'll be here seven days," Grandpa said.

"One whole week!" Aidan said. Their RV trip had really brought home the idea of a calendar since they had recently decided that for the rest of the trip they would stay in each state for exactly one month.

"We're staying at Billie and Bobbie's house while we're here. They had a last minute cancellation on their guest room."

"It was such a coincidence!" Bobbie said.

"Pretty much everyone in town takes on boarders during the Sturgis Motorcycle Rally since there aren't enough campsites to accommodate the huge crowds that come here," Billie said. "We'd had our room booked since last year."

"But the people cancelled right on the very day your grandparents wanted a place." Bobbie finished Billie's sentence, as she often did.

"Freaky awesome for us!" Aidan said as he hugged his grandma. "I've missed you so much!"

Wright 🐢n Time

"This is so exciting!" Nadia said. "What all are you going to do?"

"Mostly visit with you," Grandpa said. "But Grandma and I will have to find time to go to the Rally. I can't wait to see the new motorcycle add-ons."

"And I'm sure we'll find time to go swimming and hiking with you too," Grandma added.

"And we," Harrison said, "will also be taking a tour of Bobbie's newspaper today. She is the owner and publisher of it."

"I've always wanted to see a newspaper being printed!" Nadia said.

"But first, we're going hunting for gold!" Grandma said.

"Gold?" Aidan asked with a huge grin.

Grandma and Grandpa smiled and nodded. They had missed their grandchildren's enthusiasm for everything.

SOUTH DAKOTA

Chapter Five

Starting in the trailhead parking area, Billie led the way. With hiking boots on and a water bottle at her side, she was ready to tackle any mountain or stream. The land was green with pine trees and the dirt was black. The pine scent was strong in the air and everything felt fresh and clean. It looked completely different than the Arizona and Utah mountains the Wrights had recently explored. Those were red and rocky.

Wright ✸n Time

These mountains were just as fascinating and beautiful, just in a completely different way.

Aidan held Grandma's hand as they followed Billie up the well-worn path. Nadia and Grandpa wandered in a different direction, looking at placards that explained what all the various vegetation was. Nadia was always drawn to signs, no matter what they said. Aidan liked to charge ahead.

Stephanie caught up to Billie. "This definitely feels like we're climbing a mountain," she said.

"We are," Billie said.

"Then why are the Black Hills called hills rather than Black Mountains?"

"When you look at them from a distance, they look like rolling black hills. All the ponderosa pine trees together look very black from a distance."

"How high are they?" Stephanie asked.

"Believe it or not, the Black Hills are actually the highest elevation east of the Rocky Mountains in the United States. They are even taller than the Appalachians."

SOUTH DAKOTA

"Wow, I had no idea! So, what brought you to live here?"

"There are many aspects to these mountains and the area which drew my sister and me to live here. I'm a Native American archeologist and Bobbie, as you know, runs one of our local newspapers. Our grandpa, and great-grandpa before him, actually owned the newspaper that she owns now, but we never lived here until about five years ago. We both do a lot of hiking, too. The area is perfect for all kinds of outdoor activities."

Harrison caught the tail end of the women's conversation. He joined in. "We're wanting to study archeology more on our travels. We've been going to places where there is a lot of history."

By then, Aidan and Grandma had caught up too.

"I didn't even realize modern day archeologists existed," Grandma said.

"Indiana Jones isn't a myth!" Aidan said.

"But, we aren't all searching for the Ark of the Covenant," Billie said. "That's the myth part."

Wright ❀n Time

She smiled. "I help find and date pottery shards, cave drawings, and arrowheads, mostly. Other items, too, of course."

"Cave drawings?" Aidan asked.

"Yes, there are a lot of Native American drawings in this area."

"My sister will be excited to hear that," Aidan said. "She loves to decipher petroglyphs and hieroglyphs. She's even been researching Chinese and Japanese characters lately."

"That sounds fun!" Billie said. "I'll have to talk to her about that later."

The party continued climbing. Grandpa and Nadia caught up.

"Are we in the Black Hills National Forest?" Nadia asked.

"No. We're really close, but this is actually private land. I've been finding a lot of arrowheads here lately," Billie said. The young woman bent down and picked up some dirt. "This was an ideal place for Native Americans to live. The soil is good and lots of animals have always lived here. We can read about their stories in the cave and rock drawings. Native Americans still live in this area. It is a very important place for their culture and heritage."

They reached a peak and stopped. The sun came out from behind a cloud and suddenly the entire valley sparkled.

"Diamonds!" Aidan gasped.

"No, it's fairy dust!" Nadia said as she nudged Grandma. The two shared a love of all things related to fairies.

"I think so!" Grandma said.

They stood and stared at the glittering landscape. After a long minute, Billie interrupted their thoughts. "Actually, it's mica."

She took a few steps, then bent down to pick up a tiny piece. It broke in half as she handed it to Aidan. The opaque flakes were as thin as tissue paper and crackled like it, too. Billie saw the hesitation in everyone's eyes. They were afraid to walk on the fragile mica.

"It's okay. Go ahead. Most of it isn't as fragile as that piece." She picked up a large rock. It, too, was sparkly and shone in the sunlight.

Wright ✖ n Time

The blue and pink colors in the mica were surprising to Aidan. "Freaky wow!" he said. "Does everything shine like gold here?"

"It certainly seems like it sometimes," Billie said solemnly. "The Black Hills are a mystical and magical place for many people, me included."

"I can see why!" Nadia said.

"Real gold is actually what brought settlers to the area in the late 1800s," Billie continued. "There was a gold rush to the Black Hills and the government kicked Native Americans out in the process, which was a bad thing. Gold and silver mines were introduced then and they've continued to find millions of dollars' worth of gold and silver every year without fail. Black Hills gold is very unique. You'll probably see a lot of jewelry at the Rally with Black Hills gold. It often has colored grape leaves on it, and is called tri-colored jewelry."

"What are the colors?" Nadia asked.

"Here, see my ring?" Billie said as she held out her hand. "Pink and green leaves on a yellow gold band."

SOUTH DAKOTA

"It's beautiful," Nadia said. "How can gold be different colors?"

"Yes, it is. The colors are made from alloys. That's when you add metals to other metals. The pink and green are made when copper and silver are added to the pure gold found here in the Black Hills."

"Freaky cool!" Aidan said. "I want to find some."

"I don't think you'll find real gold here, but you never know," Billie said.

Harrison and Stephanie were happy. Being happy and enjoying the scenery as a family was their entire reason for wanting to bring their family to the area.

They scattered and explored the landscape.

"I found gold!" Aidan hollered with a laugh a few minutes later.

They congregated around Aidan. He smiled at them.

"I actually found iron pyrite," he said. "I know it's really just Fool's Gold. But, honestly, I love it more than real gold." He hugged it to his body. "See! It's much more sparkly." He held up the rock for his family to see.

"If you look around, you'll find lots and lots of iron pyrite around here. You can each take a piece. I have permission from the owner to take samples. On public land you wouldn't be able to take any," Billie told them.

No other words had to be said. They were all searching now. After they had all found some Fool's Gold they didn't want to part with, they slowly made their way back to their vehicles.

SOUTH DAKOTA

Chapter Six

Back in Sturgis, Bobbie opened the glass door of her business from the inside and ushered the Wright family into the building. Grandpa and Grandma came along for the tour, while Billie went to work at her booth at the Rally. Today was the first official day of the Rally and Billie was excited to open her booth, where she was selling postcards featuring her own photography. The roar of motorcycles and loud music could be heard from the entrance of the newspaper building. Since the building was at the edge of town, though, only a handful of riders could be seen, giving the barest of hints of the grandness of the event going on a half mile away.

"Welcome! Welcome!" Bobbie said.

She locked the door behind the guests and ushered them past the reception area into her office.

"Here, Harrison." Bobbie handed him some papers. "Sorry they are all printouts rather than electronic. We'll be almost completely digital in another year or so, but it's a long process."

Harrison took the papers and put them into his backpack. They'd be enormously helpful to him in researching the history of the Sturgis Motorcycle Rally for his upcoming article. Bobbie turned from Harrison and smiled at the rest of the family.

"Who here has seen a newspaper being printed before?" Bobbie asked. Only Grandpa, Grandma, and Harrison had.

"Okay, then," Bobbie stood and pushed open her office door. "The first thing you are going to notice once we get into the press room is the noise!"

She cracked open the press room door to let them hear the sound a little bit. They all winced slightly at the roar of the machinery. Nadia stuck her fingers in her ears to block out the rhythmic pounding.

Bobbie smiled and closed the door. She handed Stephanie a small baggie. "Before I forget, here are some earplugs for all of you. You'll need these later on our tour. Many of our employees here wear them all the time. It helps their hearing long term. It's not as loud as a really loud rock concert, so your exposure wouldn't cause permanent hearing problems. It might give you a bit of ringing in your ears for a while though. It'll get you all ready for the music at the Rally." She laughed again, sounding much like her sister.

"Should we put them in now?" Stephanie asked, starting to hand them out and show Nadia and Aidan how to roll the earplugs between their fingers to insert them properly. She handed Aidan a pair first since he was so anxious. He had loved wearing earplugs whenever he had gone indoor skydiving with his dad.

"I'll let you know when it's time for earplugs. We have a bunch of other rooms to go to first," Bobbie said.

"Okay." Stephanie put the bag of earplugs into her camera bag.

"What did she say?" Aidan asked. He had put the earplugs in as soon as he got them and hadn't heard a thing since. Grandma tapped him on the shoulder and pointed to her ears. Aidan took the hint and removed his earplugs. "Oh," he said with a grin.

Bobbie led them past the press room door, down a narrow hallway, and into a long skinny room that was not much larger than a walk-in closet. The room was dim with the appearance of no windows. Nadia squinted and noticed that there really were windows, but they were covered with black paper and black mini-blinds. She wondered if they were covered so that there wouldn't be as much glare on the screens of all the computers in the room.

SOUTH DAKOTA

A young brown-haired man was sitting at a long table. The table had five large computer monitors and three chairs sharing the space. The man heard the group come into his private area and he swiveled around on his desk chair, nodding in greeting.

"Meet Jim," Bobbie said holding out her hand toward the man. "Jim is our layout guy. He is the master here and we all bow to his creative perfection."

Jim nodded again and a bright red blush covered his face. It seemed that he took praise modestly. "Hi," he said shyly.

Bobbie knew Jim's shyness and continued for him. "This room is called the composing room, and does double duty as our news room. Newspaper articles used to be typed up and then laid out on special paper to make them fit on the pages. There are also photographs and advertisements to be put in."

She pointed to an old newspaper framed on the wall. "That's what was done when this paper was first printed over a hundred years ago."

Wright ☠n Time

"Wow! Is that a copy of your first paper?" Nadia asked.

"Yes, it is. Things have obviously changed over the years. We're still a small press with a small circulation, and the theory of newspaper layout is the same, but now almost everything is done on computers. This makes our time a lot more efficient. We only need to have one layout person instead of the three the paper had when I was a kid. My grandpa ran the paper back then and I loved to visit and have him show me around."

Bobbie looked nostalgic for a moment and then pointed to the various computer monitors on the long table against the wall.

"Our staff writers and photographers send their articles in, they are edited by me, and then Jim lets me know where each would fit best and in what size column. He's the master of filling in all the blank spaces and fitting everything in the paper in the most efficient and readable manner."

"Doesn't sound hard," Aidan said.

"It sounds really straightforward, doesn't it?" She laughed. "Jim and I should be reminded of that right before print time, huh, Jim? Seems like there is always a time crunch then."

Jim blushed again and stifled a little laugh. "Yeah, it does sound easy, but there is a real art to it. There are a lot of details that most people don't even think about. Even one extra word in an article can mess up the layout on a whole paper."

"Never Jim's fault though, of course. Always mine."

Bobbie patted Jim on the shoulder and laughed her bubbly laugh again. The Wright family was starting to realize that while the twin sisters looked alike, their personalities were a lot different. Billie was a serious scientist, though she did joke around a bit. It was Bobbie who had the laugh which could be heard for miles. It was contagious.

Bobbie showed them a few sample articles and how the layout program worked. Aidan got impatient and started squirming. Noticing this, Grandma invited Aidan to join her in finding a drink of water while everyone else learned the intricacies of newspaper layout.

Chapter Seven

"This must be the break room," Grandma said to Aidan as they walked into a room full of small round tables and simple chairs. A full kitchen lined the wall. Aidan made a beeline to the water cooler.

The two sat at one of the small round tables to drink their water. They found a large roll of paper that had a bunch of doodles and odd games on it. There were also several pens, so they played a few games of tic-tac-toe while they waited for the rest of the tour.

"And, this is our break room."

They could hear Bobbie talking in the hallway.

"We also have a gazebo out back where anyone can go to have a break or eat lunch or whatever."

"What's a gazebo?" Aidan asked his grandma.

"It's like a ramada," she said. It was the first time Grandma realized how much growing up in Arizona had affected Aidan's vocabulary, and she was excited by all the new things he was going to be learning about on his travels.

Bobbie led the group through the break room toward the other entrance to the press room at the far end.

"Before we go into the press room, I want to tell you a bit more about the process it takes for pure information to turn into a newspaper. There are several really important parts to running a newspaper that all editors have to keep in mind," Bobbie continued, making sure she had everyone's attention. "It's a fairly straightforward process, so I'll try to keep it simple."

"That's good," Grandma said as she smiled at Aidan. "If you get bored," she whispered to him, "we'll go outside and play."

"Okay," Aidan replied, giving his grandma's hand a squeeze.

"I think he'll really like seeing the paper being printed and put together," Grandpa said to her.

"Okay," Bobbie started again. "I've already shown you the layout room…"

"And the break room," Aidan added.

"And the break room," Bobbie agreed. "Now I'm going to show you the really fun to see areas."

"All right!" Nadia said.

"Now, everything is a bit more hectic than usual right now. We are normally a weekly paper. This means we only put out one paper a week——on Sundays. However, with the Sturgis Motorcycle Rally, we are putting out two extra papers over the next week. So, we've hired on additional help and the press is printing more than usual. I've invited you here right now so you can see it all in action."

Aidan stood and joined his parents. This did indeed sound exciting to him.

"Back to where we were before, most newspapers have a press room where all the reporters and editors work to write their articles. But, since we are a small paper, it's pretty much just me and a few reporters who work from their homes and send in their articles. Those articles come directly to me first, and I edit them in my office or at home on my computer there. Once I am happy with the final article, it is sent over to Jim for the layout. You've already seen how that works. Any questions so far?"

Everyone shook their heads no, so Bobbie continued. Nadia and Harrison both jotted down a few notes in the notebooks they always kept with them.

"Alrighty then, let's go see the paper actually getting made. Now would be a good time for you to put in your earplugs."

As the family worked on putting their earplugs in, Bobbie continued, raising her voice much louder. "After Jim composes the pages, they each get photographed by a special scanning machine and printed onto large thin sheets of aluminum metal. I'm not going to show you that since it is being used right now and there are a lot of fragile materials in that area. Those sheets of metal are then put onto big cylinders which are attached onto the press machine. They then get ink rolled onto them, which transfers to a rubber cylinder. That rubber cylinder presses against the paper that rolls past, leaving the ink on the paper to show all the words and pictures."

"What do the rolls of paper look like?" Nadia asked, practically screaming.

"Are all your earplugs in?" Bobbie asked.

Everyone nodded. The press machine wasn't on right that minute, but they still couldn't hear much with their earplugs in place.

"Okay, let's go see the rolls then." Bobbie opened the press room door and they all stepped in the large cavernous room. "Here is one of the rolls of paper we use." She indicated a roll of paper that had a diameter about the same height as Aidan.

Wright 🐢n Time

"This is paper?" Aidan asked with wide eyes. "Freaky wow! It's almost as big as me!"

"Yes, that is called newsprint. We need a lot of newsprint when we print a lot of news." Bobbie laughed. "A roll of newsprint is about three and a half feet tall and gives us over 35,000 feet of paper."

"Thirty-five thousand feet?" Harrison said, prepared to write down the answer.

"Isn't that, like, over five or six miles?" Nadia asked.

Stephanie did some quick calculating. "Over six and three-quarters."

"Freaky wow!" Aidan said, imagining the newsprint laid out straight for almost seven miles —nearly his age. "It'd go on forever."

"How much does it weigh?" Nadia asked.

"Between eight and nine hundred pounds."

"Oh, my!" Harrison said.

"Freaky awesome! It could squish me!" Aidan said.

"Yes, it could." Bobbie nodded.

"Do you always use up the whole roll?" Grandma asked.

SOUTH DAKOTA

"No, we almost never do, actually. We use as much as we can, and then stop the roll before the end so that it doesn't break. I noticed that you and Aidan found a nearly empty roll in the break room. You were playing tic-tac-toe on some of the leftover newsprint. We usually give the ends of the rolls to schools or churches or employees. Kids just love it for drawing on."

"Can we have some?" Aidan asked.

"Certainly. Remind me before you go and I'll grab you a few rolls on my way home today."

"Thanks!" Nadia and Aidan both said, thinking of all the fun things they could do with such a large piece of paper.

"So, where was I?" Bobbie asked herself. "Oh, yes. These huge rolls of paper get put on the press and the sheet of paper rolls past all those plates and rollers until the whole paper has been printed onto it."

She led them closer to the machine, which wasn't running at that moment.

"Then the pages get cut apart and folded together by another machine. This happens thousands of times over and over again until we have the exact number of papers we want."

Bobbie pointed at the parts of the huge machine as she talked about them. "The folded papers are then put onto this conveyor belt. As you can see, the conveyor winds around and around and runs clear up into the ceiling."

Just then, the man in charge of the press started it going again. A loud bell rang, indicating that everyone should watch out for the moving parts on the machines.

"What are those red buttons?" Aidan shouted. It was now very noisy and they all had to yell to be heard.

"Those are emergency buttons," Bobbie said.

"Red usually means emergency," Stephanie added.

"If something is wrong with the press or a conveyor belt, or if anyone has their clothing, hair, or body stuck in a machine, then any of the red buttons can be pushed and everything will instantly stop."

"Wow!" Aidan said.

SOUTH DAKOTA

"Has that ever happened?" Nadia asked.

"The machine does get jammed a lot..." Bobbie started.

"With people?" Aidan exclaimed, freaked out at the thought.

"Never with people, knock on wood," Bobbie said as she found a close doorframe to physically knock on. "We are a very safe press. Our jams are mostly paper jams."

They all stood in awe, watching the press run.

"How many papers can it print in an hour?" Grandpa asked.

"At full speed, it can print nearly thirty thousand per hour," Bobbie said. "But, we don't usually need that many, so we don't usually run it that fast."

Once the guests were done watching the print machine, Bobbie continued the tour.

"So let's go in the next room and see what happens next." She began pointing again. "This is the mail room. There is that same conveyor belt. It is bringing the printed newspapers into this room. Here, they go into a machine called a stacker. This, as you would expect, stacks up the papers into bundles."

The machine and the workers were working hard. The family tried very carefully to not get in anyone's way. They'd noticed yellow lines painted like sidewalks on the ground when they had first walked into the press room and they had automatically stayed within them.

Bobbie pointed again. "Those stacks of papers run along this conveyor belt to our inserting machine. This might seem like a boring part, but it is the most essential part of our newspaper. It is how we make money."

The workers working on the machines glanced at Bobbie and smiled. They were all friends and were happy to be working on such a wonderful paper. The Wrights were all quiet as they took it all in.

"The people working here put the papers into the inserting machine along with advertisements from outside companies. The machine sticks the ads into the paper a lot faster than a person could do it. We receive advertisement money for every ad we insert. We get a lot more money from ads than we do from the amount we charge per paper. From that money, we can pay the employees and pay for the expenses of running the business."

Bobbie continued walking ahead.

"This next machine stacks the papers up again and wraps a plastic band around them to hold the stack together in bundles. It is important that the stack is always about the same thickness. Too thin and the papers rip. Too thick and the strap won't fit. But that means that we need to stack different numbers of papers depending on how thick they are. It all depends on how much news was printed that day."

"How thick is a bundle?" Nadia asked.

"About a foot," Bobbie said.

"That's twelve inches, right?" Aidan asked.

"Yes," Stephanie said.

"How many papers are usually in a bundle?" Nadia asked.

"It really does vary, but it's usually between thirty and forty. Ours is a thin paper. This week it'll be about twenty because we have a lot more news and advertising during the Rally."

"Seventeen today," said a man working on the line.

"Seventeen! Lots of news today," Bobbie said.

"More like lots of inserts," said a woman working on the line.

"Good for us!" Bobbie said as she smiled at them. "It's looking great today."

Bobbie continued walking past the inserter.

"Here is another conveyor belt. This one takes the stacked-up papers over to Al, who makes sure that the right number of bundles are set aside for each delivery route. He also makes sure the right stacks get on the trucks as they pull up to our loading dock here. This is usually done in the middle of the night on Saturday night, so the paper can be on the doorsteps of all our Sunday morning readers. But, you can see that it is being done early today. This is a special evening edition paper for the first day of the Rally."

"How many routes do you have?" Harrison asked, pen in hand.

SOUTH DAKOTA

"Usually only a dozen drivers. Those drivers fill up the backs of their trucks and take stacks of papers to the individual carriers. In a big paper, this is managed by a circulation department. Here, it's just Betty and me."

"Who is Betty?" Grandma asked.

"Oh, I don't think you got to meet her. Betty is our receptionist and all-around 'pick up the pieces' woman. We wouldn't be able to run this newspaper without her."

"How many routes will you have for tonight's paper?" Nadia asked.

"I don't know. Al," Bobbie called over to the man on the dock. "How many routes tonight?"

"Same ol'," he said. "Most are goin' straight to our booth at the Rally."

"That makes sense," Harrison said. "Taking them straight to the buyers."

"How do out-of-town people get their papers?" Stephanie asked.

"Bundles of out-of-town papers are considered a route of their own. They get taken to Betty; she wraps them all up and mails them all out. Like I said, she really picks up a lot of slack. She also takes down all the personal ad information, although we have an accountant who takes care of billing. Betty's got extra help this week, though, as a lot of readers want our special Rally editions. Her daughters, who are home from college, are helping. It's a big job for the few weeks before, during, and after the Rally."

Bobbie led them back through the press room and into the reception area again. Betty was nowhere in sight. They took out their earplugs and threw them away.

"Throwing those away seems like a waste," Nadia commented, "especially if everyone does that every day."

"True," Bobbie said. "You might not have noticed, but all the employees have their own earplugs that are reusable. We only use the throw-away kind for guests, and we're looking into finding biodegradable ones for those."

"Clever," Grandma said.

"Well, that's about it," Bobbie said. "Any questions about how a newspaper is printed?"

SOUTH DAKOTA

They all shook their heads no.

"Don't hesitate to ask me later if you think of something," she said. "I'll be sure to bring a few rolls of newsprint home tonight. I've got to get going right now, but I'll have the paper at my house for you to pick up anytime later this week."

"Thank you!" they all said to Bobbie.

"You're all very welcome!"

"I'll be e-mailing you my final article by tomorrow night," Harrison told Bobbie.

"Great. That'll be perfect timing for the next edition. If you want to write a second article about family-friendly things to do in the area, that would be great."

"Good idea! I'll do that."

"Have fun tonight at the Rally."

"We will!" the kids said.

They all left the building. Bobbie locked the door behind them. Since they'd already parked their cars at Billie and Bobbie's house, the group walked the few blocks to the Rally.

Chapter Eight

"Welcome to the infamous Sturgis Motorcycle Rally," Billie said to the Wright family and Grandpa and Grandma as they stepped up to the front of the queue at Billie's booth.

She was too busy with customers to have a full conversation.

"Have a flag tattoo."

She pointed to a large wicker basket behind her. It was full of thousands of little temporary

Wright✼n Time

United States flag tattoos. They were a free giveaway for her customers, or perhaps anyone who came to her booth.

Billie smiled at everyone who came to her booth. She was selling postcards with photographs of her Harley motorcycle and sidecar in front of various South Dakota landmarks. Many weren't famous, but all were gorgeous. People could also get their pictures taken sitting on her motorcycle right there at the stand.

Grandma picked up a postcard and looked at it closely. "Wow, these are beautiful," she said. "And you take them yourself?"

"Every single one here," Billie said proudly. She spread out her arm indicating the table and racks of postcards. "I spend a lot of time in the hills and I love my camera. I have even more at home in case I sell out of these."

Aidan was looking over her motorcycle, admiring the flames.

"Go ahead and climb in the sidecar. I'll take your picture," Billie said.

"Really? Freaky cool!" Aidan said.

SOUTH DAKOTA

"Can I, too?" asked Nadia.

"That's what it's here for. Why don't all four of you get on? I'll take a family photo," Billie responded.

The Wrights put on the goggles and other props that Billie had left for customers to use. They all smiled for the camera, especially Aidan, who had always wanted to be on a motorcycle.

"Wave at me," Grandpa said.

Billie snapped the photo and then turned to deal with another customer, who was interested in the postcards.

"Every postcard comes with a stamp and I'll personally make sure it's postmarked within a day," she told him.

The leather-clad man grabbed a bunch and paid her.

"Drop off the written postcards whenever you like and I'll mail them for you. Here's a pen if you want to write something now."

"Got a sunset postcard?" a lady asked Billie.

"Several," she said. "Check these out over here." Billie pointed to an entire rack of spectacular sunset views.

"Thanks," the lady replied as she went to pick out a couple.

"Seems like you are doing good business," Harrison said.

"I'm pleased," Billie said. "You should go and check out the artists down there." She pointed to an area a block away where several artists had drawn admiring crowds.

"When can I see the photograph you took of us on your motorcycle?" Aidan asked, noticing that Billie was free to talk again.

"I'll have all the photos I took today online later tonight. You can download any that you want for free," Billie said.

"Freaky cool!" Aidan said, excited to have a picture of himself on a motorcycle. He couldn't wait to e-mail it to his best friend Connor.

"Thanks. Sounds good," Stephanie said.

"See you later!" Nadia and Aidan said, reaching for their grandparents' hands.

"Sell out!" Grandpa told her, wishing her good luck.

"Have fun!" Grandma said.

SOUTH DAKOTA

"You too!" Billie called as they walked away from her booth.

The talented artists were painting anything and everything on various motorcycle parts and helmets. One was even painting on leather jackets and chaps. Some were drawing freehand, others were using stencils. All were using special paints designed for the project they were painting.

Aidan was drawn to a spray painting artist who seemed to create new designs with no effort at all. Aidan knew if he had been the one wielding the paint, it never would have looked like anything other than random color blotches.

"That's freaky awesome!" Aidan said to Grandma, pointing at how two quick sprays produced a coyote on a canvas in seconds.

"It's just unreal," she agreed.

Wright ✺n Time

On their walk from one booth to another, they found out that many of the artists' services were so desired that their time had been booked a year or more in advance. A few of the newer artists still had sign up times available. Many had a helper who explained the process to prospective customers.

"Marsha would want your motorcycle for a six hour block for that design," one helper was saying to a potential customer.

Nadia didn't like large crowds, yet she wanted to see the artists work so she held her dad's hand tightly and they slowly made their way through the crowd together. She became more and more nervous the closer they got to the actual artists. Each of the artists had a rope indicating how close the crowd was allowed to get. It was great for the artists working, but made for large crowds right up against the roped-off areas.

Nadia usually liked to doodle or take notes whenever she felt nervous, but that wasn't possible in a large throng of people, so she did the next best thing. She put her hand in her pocket and fiddled with the object she found there—the Time Tuner. She rubbed it as though it were a worry stone, absentmindedly stroking the object in circles. The more her thumb moved, the harder she squeezed Harrison's hand. Stephanie and Aidan were right in front of her, holding hands. Grandpa and Grandma had stepped to the side to check out a stand selling a special paint that was used on motorcycles.

Nadia felt lightheaded in the crowd. She gently tugged her dad's hand down so he'd know to put his ear to her mouth.

"I'm thirsty," she whispered as she continued to stroke the object in her pocket.

"All right, we'll go find something to drink," he said to her.

Harrison tapped his wife on the shoulder. When she didn't respond, he let his hand rest on her shoulder. He knew that would get her attention.

Suddenly, time stopped around the four Wrights.

Chapter Nine

Shockingly, all sound and movement stopped around the Wrights, who simultaneously gasped.

Stephanie was the first to speak. "What's going on?" she said, as she swirled around to face Harrison and Nadia. She clutched tighter to Aidan, afraid he would get hurt. She grabbed at Harrison with her free hand, putting them in a U-shape.

"I don't know," Harrison replied.

Wright ✦n Time

"Freaky wow," Aidan said as he looked around them at all the statue-still people.

Nadia's face went completely white.

"Look!" Aidan said, trying to break his mother's grasp.

"Don't let go of my hand," Stephanie said. Fear was in her voice and Aidan knew she was serious.

"But at least look!" Aidan pointed with his free hand to the spray painting artist.

Droplets of red paint were suspended in the air.

"And look at that man on the motorcycle!" Aidan pointed to a man in the distance who had been jumping his motorcycle over a ramp. He, too, was suspended in mid-air.

The other three gasped as they took in all the sights Aidan had already seen.

"What has happened to us?" Harrison asked.

"I really don't know," Stephanie answered.

"I think I do," Nadia said quietly.

Her family all looked at her. She pulled the Time Tuner out of her pocket and held it up. It felt stuck in her hand, as if she could have let go and it wouldn't have left her grasp. She wasn't sure, though, and wasn't about to test the theory.

"The Time Tuner!" Aidan said. "It really does tune time, doesn't it?"

Nadia looked apprehensive. "I was nervous and it was in my pocket," she started.

"And you were touching it?" Stephanie asked.

Nadia nodded. "I wasn't even thinking."

She brought the device close to her face and noted that the symbols were all blue. Other than that, it looked the same as it usually did.

"It's all right, don't worry," Harrison said. He wanted to draw her closer and hug her, but he was afraid to let go of her hand. He was afraid to let go of Stephanie, too. "We don't know the effects of what is going on, but we were all touching each other when it happened," he said.

"So we should probably not let go of each other," Stephanie said. She tried to sound calm, but Harrison could tell she was still frightened.

"But it's going to be fine. I'm sure of it," Harrison said as he smiled at Stephanie.

Wright ✹n Time

Nadia didn't know whether to cry or be stoic, so she stayed silent—thinking hard about how to get them out of this crazy predicament.

"Really," Harrison said to Nadia, noting her unusual quietness. "Remember Prince Pumpkin the Third this morning? Everything was fine there. I think we are just discovering, like Aidan said already, that our little Time Tuner has properties of tuning time. We really have named it appropriately."

This cheered Nadia up and she gave a little reluctant smile. "But it's all my fault." Tears sprang to her eyes.

"Not fault," Harrison said. "It's all your discovery!" He seemed proud. "Really, this is super cool!"

"No, freaky cool!" Aidan said.

"That's true, freaky cool!" Harrison agreed.

Even Stephanie started warming up at this and she smiled back at Harrison.

"But how do we make it stop?" Nadia asked.

SOUTH DAKOTA

"I think you mean, how do we make it go," Stephanie said, nodding at the still crowds around them.

"Who cares?!" Aidan said. He started pulling on Stephanie's hand. "For now, let's go explore!"

The parents couldn't think of anything better to do, so they followed Aidan's lead. He dragged his family through the throng of Rally attendees.

"Slow down!" Nadia hollered to him. "I'm banging into people."

"Yeah, your mom and I are a bit bigger than you, too," Harrison said, laughing. "We don't want to push anyone over, or worse yet, a motorcycle." The thought of pushing over a motorcycle made him look around himself even more carefully.

Aidan slowed down and took a left through the side of a booth onto the sidewalk. He wove his family through the crowds and booths, stepping around barricades, and was soon right underneath the flying motorcycle.

"Check this out!" Aidan said.

Wright 🐢 n Time

"Is this safe?" Stephanie asked.

"I'm sure it's fine," Harrison replied. "Just don't move your fingers or thumb on that device anymore, Nadia."

"I won't." Nadia shook her head solemnly.

"Then let's have some fun!" Harrison said.

Aidan squirmed around while Stephanie kept a strong hold on his hand. He led them through the motorcycle ramps and into the side streets. He stopped suddenly and pointed. A little bird was mid-flight with its mouth wide open, about to catch a bug. The family stared with their own mouths wide open as they continued to follow Aidan around the trees, cars, motorcycles, and people.

"I want to lead," Nadia said as she tugged on the chain, drawing them to a stop. Her voice was clear and loud in the eerie silence that surrounded them. "I want to go and see the artists' works without the big crowd," she said.

Even Aidan agreed that would be fun to do, so Nadia led the chain back to the Rally and they carefully walked inside the roped-off art areas.

SOUTH DAKOTA

"Look at this one," Stephanie said as she pointed with her head. "Those flames are amazing."

"I like seeing the paint in mid-air," Aidan said, reaching to touch a bubble of paint in the air.

"I'd love to get a photograph of that!" Stephanie said. With all the incredible things they'd witnessed, she was itching to take the camera out of her pocket. Unfortunately, both of her hands were occupied.

"Wouldn't that be amazing!" Nadia said.

"Think you could get my camera out of my pocket, Aidan?" Stephanie asked him. "You are the only one with a free hand."

Aidan saw the camera strap for his mom's small point-and-shoot camera sticking out of her pocket and he tugged on it with his free left hand. "Got it." He put it close to his other hand and carefully pushed the on button. Aidan was determined, but, being right-handed, had a hard time using his left hand to hold the camera and click the button to take photos. He took a few and they all decided that would have to do.

Wright ✺n Time

They continued weaving in and out of all the art booths. As they neared where the adventure had begun, Nadia asked Harrison what he wanted to see.

"Maybe some people eating," he laughed. "Or, perhaps a dog running…"

"My hand is sweaty," Aidan interrupted.

Before Stephanie could do anything about it, he'd slipped out of her grasp. Instantly, with the connection broken, time restarted, noise and movements and all.

"I'm so sorry!" Aidan said to his family, realizing what had happened. He was inches from a woman he almost tripped. "Excuse me," he said to the passing woman.

"Oh well!" Harrison said, going with the flow.

"At least it didn't happen when we were under that motorcycle!" Stephanie cried, fear back in her voice.

With the sudden return of crowd noise, all four of them shook their heads at the loudness.

"It doesn't feel stuck anymore," Nadia said, referring to the device in her hand. She examined the Time Tuner without touching it to see whether anything had changed. Other than the quickly fading blue tinge, it looked like it usually did. Within seconds, it was completely back to normal.

Nadia let go of her dad's hand and wiped her own on her jeans. She, too, had a sweaty hand. None of them usually held hands for that long.

Harrison bent his head to look at the Time Tuner. Nadia offered it to him and he took it in his hand and examined it from all angles.

"Where'd you all go?" Grandma suddenly said. She and Grandpa had joined them. The Wrights were about ten feet away from where they had been when time had stopped.

"You were there one second, then the next thing we knew, you were all gone," Grandpa said.

"You're all so quick!" Grandma said. "But don't freak Grandma out like that!"

Somehow this all seemed ridiculously silly and all four Wrights doubled over in laughter. Between gasps, they relayed their time adventure to the shocked and amazed looks of their grandparents. People passing noted their happiness, but in the party atmosphere of the Rally, there was nothing unusual about people laughing together. Everyone was *supposed* to be having fun.

"Hey, look, Nadia! There's the bird again!" Aidan hollered, pointing to it.

"He caught the bug!" Nadia noted, glad to see that everything had resumed normally. The experience had been like having a remote control with a pause button for the entire world. She was already thinking of ways they could use this new Time Tuner feature in the future, if only she could figure out how she had triggered it.

SOUTH DAKOTA

Crazy Horse, South Dakota

The Black Hills
South Dakota

The Badlands

Chapter Ten

Harrison stayed at the Rally so he could interview people for his stories. Stephanie stayed to take photographs. The rest of the family went back to the house so they could eat a quiet dinner and get some much-needed time alone together.

Nadia and Aidan sat at Bobbie and Billie's dining table with their grandparents. They'd been able to find Native American tacos—made of fry bread, beans, lettuce, tomatoes, and salsa—and lemon shake-ups at the Rally. The long walks they'd had that day had made them all feel like they were starving.

"Don't get too full," Grandma said. "Grandpa made brownies!"

"Oh, yum, my favorite," Nadia said.

"I can't believe all the tents we saw." Aidan said, referring to the front lawns and backyards in the neighborhood around Billie and Bobbie's house. Not only had the residents rented out their extra rooms, but they'd rented out their yards and RVs, too.

"I know!" Nadia said. "Bobbie said their newspaper usually only has a circulation of about five thousand and the town's population is just under seven thousand. Yet, this week their circulation will be two *hundred* thousand! I just can't believe it."

"Yes, there might be more people here in this little town today than the number of people who live in the entire state," Grandpa said.

"Freaky awesome!" Aidan said.

"It's no wonder Billie's booth is doing so well. I hope she sells out," Grandma said.

SOUTH DAKOTA

"I bought five of her postcards. They are so cool. Look at this one," Nadia said as she held out a particular card. "It's a photo of exactly where Aidan found the Fool's Gold earlier today. I'm sending that one to you, Grandma!"

"That's weird. She's here! Grandma doesn't want a postcard of somewhere she's been," Aidan said.

"Oh, that's especially what I want a postcard of. I will love to receive it when I get home, Nadia. I will look at it and it'll remind me of this day. What a wonderful thought." Grandma reached over and squeezed Nadia's hand and stroked her hair. She was happy she was seeing her granddaughter in person.

"See?" Nadia said to Aidan.

"Guess I was wrong," he replied. "Think I can have one to send Connor?" Connor was Aidan's best friend from his home state of Arizona. The two liked to e-mail each other nearly every day, and Aidan sent Connor postcards and little gifts from each state the family went to. They'd been on the road for four

months and that was the longest the two had ever
been apart since the first time they'd met.

"I thought you'd want one for him," Nadia
replied. "You can have your pick of the rest."

Aidan thumbed through the postcards and
picked one of Mount Rushmore. "I know we
haven't been there yet, but we are going there,"
he said. "I wonder how big those faces are. I can't
wait to see them."

"They are sixty feet tall!" Grandpa said.
"Grandma and I went there last month. I think
you'll really like it."

"Who are the presidents?"

"George Washington, Thomas Jefferson,
Theodore Roosevelt, and Abraham Lincoln."

"Lincoln's on the penny, right?"

"Yes."

"Mom said we can go and see where he
lived when we go to Illinois."

"That will be really neat!"

"Mmm-hmm."

Grandpa told Aidan a little of the history of
Mount Rushmore as the two sat on the couch
after supper. The boy quickly fell asleep in his

SOUTH DAKOTA

lap. Grandma got out her Sudoku book and snuggled up next to Nadia. The three chatted quietly, catching up on all their separate adventures since they'd last seen each other.

Finally, Nadia showed her grandparents the Time Tuner. In Utah, they had discovered that it glowed in moonlight. But now the moon waned in the sky outside the window, and they were inside anyway, so the device looked its normal black and bronze. The young girl told them about their scare with Prince Pumpkin the Third earlier that day.

"He *is* an old turtle," Grandma said, remembering how he'd been a constant companion of hers when she had been a child.

"But everything was fine," Nadia said. "That was just another of the times we've seen really amazing things happen when the device was around." She went on to tell them about the mud and vegetables in Wyoming and the energized laptops and Internet access they had experienced in Utah.

"What curious events," Grandma said.

"And today with Prince Pumpkin the Third it was like time froze for him as he held the device. Then this evening, time was frozen for everyone who wasn't connected to the device. It was as though the same thing happened each time, but opposite."

"I've always been a firm believer that there is more to this world than what we can see," Grandpa said, looking down at the sleeping Aidan whose head was in his lap.

"Me too. I believe physicists are just beginning to explore the real truths about the universe. Perhaps the Time Tuner was made as an experiment with string theory?" Grandma wondered.

"What's string theory, Grandma?" Nadia asked.

"It's a physics theory that all energy, matter, and forces are made up of really tiny things called strings. They are smaller than particles even!"

"Wow!" Nadia exclaimed. "Mom told me that particles are smaller than atoms, so strings must be really, really tiny!"

SOUTH DAKOTA

"They are!" Grandma agreed.

"Do you really think this device might have something to do with that?" Nadia asked, holding up the Time Tuner.

"You never know," Grandpa said. "This universe is amazing."

"Let me see the Time Tuner."

Grandma set her Sudoku book and pen—she never used a pencil—down on a side table and held out her hand. She took the device from Nadia and examined it.

"I don't know whether to tell you to keep experimenting with it or to stop!" Grandma laughed. "Oh, I just worry about you so. But, it's important you never let my silly worrying get in the way of your enjoying what all this wonderful life has to offer."

"We don't, Grandma, we don't," Nadia said. She hugged her grandmother tight.

Wright ❂n Time

The drive back to the campground that night felt long and slow to the Wrights. They even had to stop once to allow a herd of bison cross the road. Stephanie was at the wheel while Harrison worked on his article in the passenger's seat. Aidan and Nadia had briefly considered staying the night with their grandparents, but changed their minds when they remembered the morning they'd had with Prince Pumpkin the Third. They wanted to wake up and see his happy face.

It had been the longest day the Wright family had ever experienced—literally. They didn't know whether they should be scared of the Time Tuner or excited by its strange abilities. Pausing time was something that seemed to defy physics and all universal laws as they understood them, but what they'd seen and experienced first hand could not be denied. First it was Prince Pumpkin the Third, then all four of them at the Rally.

Nadia knew her translating job was more important than ever. She had to decipher the symbols that seemed to randomly appear on the devicc quickly, or they'd never know what predicaments the Time Tuner would get them into next.

The kids ran into the RV the second their car stopped. They rushed to Prince Pumpkin the Third's terrarium, picked him up, and gave him a loving pat on the head.

"We missed you so much today," Aidan said. "I'll go get you some peas right now. You won't believe what we did today!"

THE END

GLOSSARY

alloy [**al**-oi]; a mixture of a metal with another element to produce a new kind of metal.

aluminum [*uh*-**loo**-mi-n*uh*m]; a light silver colored metal.

apprehensive [ap-ri-**hen**-siv]; worried about something that might happen.

Wright ✖ n Time

archeologist [ahr-kee-**ahl**-*uh*-jist]; someone who carefully studies past human life and cultures by examining found evidence.

barricade [**bar**-i-kayd]; an obstruction or barrier to keep people out of an area.

Black Hills; a small mountain range in western South Dakota extending into Wyoming.

cavernous [**kav**-er-n*uh*s]; resembling a cave.

circulation [sur-ky*uh*-**lay**-sh*uh*n]; the distribution of copies to readers.

congregated [**kong**-gri-gayt-ed]; gathered together.

contagious [k*uh*n-**tay**-j*uh*s]; spreading from one person to another.

conveyor [k*uh*n-**vay**-er]; a moving belt or chain which moves objects from one area to another.

SOUTH DAKOTA

cylinder [**sil**-in-der]; an object which is circular on two parallel ends and straight on the outside. A solid tube.

decipher [dee-**sie**-fer]; to discover the meaning of something. *Nadia helped decipher the strange markings on the mysterious device.*

diameter [die-**am**-*uh*-ter]; the distance across the widest part of a circle.

erosion [ee-**roh**-zhuhn]; wearing away due to rain, wind, or other natural forces.

freaky awesome, freaky cool, freaky weird, freaky wow; fun phrases the Wright family is popularizing. *Aidan saw a really neat object. "Freaky cool!" he said.*

gazebo [*guh*-**zee**-boh]; an open or lattice-enclosed outdoor structure with a roof, sometimes screened in; see **ramada**.

Wright 🐾n Time

habitat [**hab**-i-tat]; the place where an animal lives.

hieroglyph [**hie**-ro-glif]; a picture symbol that represents a word or idea.

Holstein [**hohl**-steen]; a breed of cow with black and white or brown and white patches of color.

homeschooled [**hohm**-skoold]; educated at home. *The Wright children are homeschooled.*

inserter [**in**-surt-er]; the machine which puts advertisements into a newspaper.

intricacy [**in**-tri-k*uh*-see]; something very detailed.

journalist [**jur**-n*uh*l-ist]; a person who writes for newspapers and magazines.

literally [**lit**-er-*uh*-lee]; what actually happened, without exaggeration.

nostalgic [n*uh*-**stal**-jic]; remembering past events in a fond way.

SOUTH DAKOTA

petroglyphs [**peh**-troh-glifs]; ancient drawings left on rocks.

physicist [**fiz**-*uh*-sist]; a scientist who specializes in physics, the science of matter, energy, motion and force.

pictograph [**pik**-t*uh*-graf]; a picture or symbol that represents a word.

pictogram [**pik**-t*uh*-gram]; see pictograph.

predicament [pri-**dik**-*uh*-ment]; a situation which is often dangerous or unpleasant.

queue [kyoo]; a line.

quizzically [**kwiz**-i-k*uh*l-lee]; in a puzzled way.

ramada [r*uh*-**mah**-d*uh*]; an open outdoor shelter, often at parks.

recreational vehicle (RV); a large vehicle that people can travel and live in. *The Wright family live in an RV.*

Wright ❀n Time

reflexively [ri-**flek**-siv-lee]; automatically, without thinking about it.

rhythmic [**rith**-mik]; having a regular beat.

speleogen [**spee**-lee-oh-jen]; a rock formation created by erosion.

speleothem [**spee**-lee-oh-thehm]; cave formation.

stoic [**stoh**-ik]; remaining unaffected in emotional situations.

Sudoku [**soo**-doh-koo]; a game of numbers in a grid.

terrarium [t*uh*-**rair**-ee-*uh*m]; a glass or plastic container for a small land animal and/or plants to live in.

Time Tuner; an amazing device the Wright family found in a salted cave in Southern Arizona, properties currently unknown.

SOUTH DAKOTA

worry stone; a special smooth rock people carry around to rub for good luck and/or calming.

MORE FACTS ABOUT SOUTH DAKOTA

- Highest Point: Harney Peak, 7244 ft above sea level
- Lowest Point: Big Stone Lake, 966 ft above sea level
- Size: 77,121 square miles (16th largest)
- Residents are called: South Dakotans
- 40th state to officially become a state
- State Motto: Under God the People Rule
- State Slogan: "Great Faces. Great Places."
- Average Rainfall: 21.3 inches per year
- Largest City: Sioux Falls
- Longest River: Missouri River
- Bordering States: Iowa, Minnesota, Montana, Nebraska, North Dakota, Wyoming
- Geographic center of the U.S. (including Alaska and Hawaii) is 17 miles west of Castle Rock, SD
- State Colors: Blue and Gold (in state flag)
- State Dessert: Kuchen
- State Grass: Western wheat grass
- State Jewelry: Black Hills gold
- State Mineral: Rose quartz
- State Musical Instrument: Fiddle
- State Name Meaning: From the Sioux language, meaning "ally" or "friend"
- State Soil: Houdek
- State Song: "Hail! South Dakota" by Deecort Hammitt

What is the image the Wright family sees on the *Time Tuner*?

In Arizona, the Wright family found a *mysterious* device which shows an image of a turtle with a special symbol in the middle. The symbol is based off of an ancient Mayan glyph called a **Hunab Ku** symbol. The Mayans believed that the symbol represented the gateway to other galaxies beyond our own sun. Only the maker of the device understands why the Hunab Ku was drawn inside of a turtle on the *Time Tuner*. Check out **www.WrightOnTimeBooks.com** and read *Wright on Time: MINNESOTA, Book 5* to find out more!

Join Nadia and Aidan on their first adventure in *Wright on Time: ARIZONA, Book 1*. There the Wrights explored a salted cave. Nadia hoped to find minerals and see rock formations. Aidan really wanted to see bats. This is the adventure where the mysterious device was found. Where was it, and what does it do? Published in August 2009.

Join Nadia and Aidan as they continue their adventures in *Wright on Time: UTAH, Book 2*. The Wrights have joined a dinosaur dig searching for allosaurus bones. Will they find any? And what will they learn about that mysterious device? Published in November 2009.

Join Nadia and Aidan in *Wright on Time: WYOMING, Book 3*. The Wrights visit geysers, tour a hydroelectric water plant, fly in a private plane, and more! What will they find and what will they learn about that mysterious device they found in Arizona? Published in August 2010.

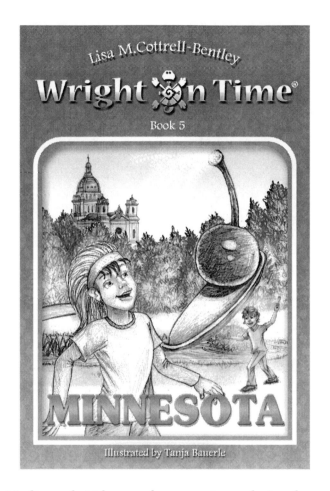

Join Nadia and Aidan as they continue their adventures in *Wright on Time: MINNESOTA, Book 5*, coming out in Summer 2011. The Wrights visit the Minneapolis Sculpture Garden and work at the Franconia Sculpture Park, all while learning about and playing with art and the *Time Tuner*.

Cody Greene and the RAINBOW MYSTERY

WRITTEN BY LINDA FIELDS

When a painting is stolen from nine year old Cody Greene's family's art gallery, he does what any artist would do: he sketches the clues. Through cooking with his friend, visiting the midwife with his mom, hiking with his dad, and helping to prepare for an upcoming art and craft festival, Cody's homeschooling takes a new turn as he unravels the Case of the Rainbow Mystery.

A Journey Through Learning

Children absorb information by using their hands. Put a lapbook into your child's hands and watch the learning begin!

A lapbook is a series of file folders glued together and loaded inside with mini-booklets. Your child records the information he/she learns inside the mini-booklets.

We carry lapbooks for all the Wright on Time books. We also have lapbooks for history, science, bible, math, literature, seasons, holidays, and early learning. Please visit our website at www.ajourneythroughlearning.com.

Tanja Bauerle at age 11 with her dog, Swift. Swift never barked and he could climb trees!

Tanja was a busy girl growing up. Born in Germany, she moved to Australia when she was 11, and later to the USA as an adult. Her favorite childhood activities were drawing and coloring. Her love for animated movies inspired her to pursue a degree in animation. Illustrators like Graeme Base and Arthur Rackham inspired her to pursue her illustrating dreams!

Check out **www.TanjaBauerle.com** for more information about Tanja and her award-winning work.

Lisa Cottrell-Bentley at age 9.5 with her favorite puzzle collection.

Lisa was born in Iowa and raised in Illinois and Iowa. She moved to Arizona as an adult. Her favorite childhood activities were writing, solving puzzles of all kinds, and dreaming up stories and creative inventions. Her love of number puzzles inspired her to pursue a degree in mathematics. Children's book authors like Beverly Cleary and Meg Cabot inspired her to pursue her writing dreams!

Check out **www.WrightOnTimeBooks.com** for more information about Lisa and her children's chapter book series.

NOTES:

NOTES:

Wright On Time®

Wright 'n Time®

CPSIA information can be obtained at www.ICGtesting.com
Printed in the USA
LVOW051432280213

322139LV00001B/153/P

9 780982 482957